G            10

# W A S T E

ellipsis
. . .
press

ISBN 0-9637536-1-4
ISBN-13 978-0-9637536-1-8

Design by Eugene Lim
Cover photograph, "Shinjuku at night" by Tanakawho
The cover photo may be copied and reproduced according to the terms set out in the Creative Commons
Attribution-ShareAlike license at http://creativecommons.org/licenses/by-sa/2.5/. The original photographic
image used for this cover can be found at http://www.flickr.com/photos/28481088@N00/2033518998/.

An excerpt of *Waste* previously appeared in *Fourteen Hills*, Volume 10 Number 2,
Summer/Fall 2004.

ELLIPSIS PRESS
www.ellipsispress.com
Brooklyn, New York

Also by Eugene Marten

*In the Blind*

W A

# STE

EUGENE MARTEN

*For Kelly—*
*if she'll have it*

THE BUILDING OWNED ITS OWN UMBRELLAS. People take advantage. They forget. They would take umbrellas back to their offices or cubicles instead of returning them at the security desk in the main lobby. It was getting to be a problem. It got so the building announced it would pay fifty cents for each returned umbrella. The next day Sloper showed up for work early. He started at the bottom and worked his way up as many floors as he could before the other janitors arrived. By the time they came after him, he'd made nearly ten dollars recovering pilfered umbrellas.

Flesh settles against bone, assuming new shapes, but Mexican is sloppier. If the tray was dumped sideways in a trash can, the guacamole and sour cream would get all over everything. The cheese skinned. The refried beans crusted into clay and the chips, all stuck together with the cheese, became soft and chewy. People never finished their chips.

Recycling went into tall white boxes that were to be picked up from the copier rooms only. Sloper used a hand truck. He didn't do favors. He wouldn't pick up from an office or a cubicle, from the aisles or the perimeters. When he got to a floor he would circle the inside perimeter surrounding the elevator lobby, but only to get to the copier rooms. It was the building's policy, he didn't want to have to explain. If an elderly employee told him the box was too heavy, Sloper told her, "Have one of the guys on the floor move it," or "Put it on your chair and roll it." People usually understand but sometimes they would complain, not just about the inconvenience but also about his terseness, or they would call him brusque, and some of those times, depending on who complained, the building would make an exception and Sloper's supervisor would brokenly tell him, "Just one time do it once."

Sometimes the boxes were so bulging with paper they couldn't be flapped, or were split down the corners. Regardless of condition, Sloper rolled them all into the freight elevator and took them down to the basement—as long as he found them where they were supposed to be, and not sitting outside someone's office or cubicle on either the inside or outside perimeter.

The supervisor was reasonable but hard to understand. She couldn't use the letter v. She walked around with a spray bottle dangling from her pocket like a side arm. A nominal assistant who'd been in the States longer made rounds with her to facilitate communication. Speaking through the supervisor via the assistant, the building told Sloper a compromise had been reached: employees would now be permitted to leave their recycling at the point on the inside perimeter nearest them, and Sloper would now be required to pick up from there as well as the copier rooms, which was okay with him since he had to go that way anyway to get to the copier rooms, as long as they understood it was on the inside and not the outside perimeter.

Still, people expect favors. They left boxes in the aisles and on the convectors, by the windows. They left little notes.

5 was a production floor. Any excuse for a party—birthdays, holidays, retirements. The floor was divided into teams. Sloper wasn't sure how they competed but if Team B beat team C there was a party. Pizza, cake and ice cream. Potluck. Your production worker never finished her food. She left feminine hygiene articles in the wastebasket right under her terminal. (The plastic applicators smelled only like plastic.) Dirty diapers. Three large cokes, each one half full. Chinese in white or transparent plastic containers. If someone was still on the floor you could secure the lid with a rubber band, slide the container under the desk, and make a mental note of its location. You were not to accept food if they offered it.

Sloper's big thick body promised great strength and he resented the obligations this seemed to confer, as certain dispositions resent the burden of physical

beauty. Once the guards fully appreciated this reti-
cence they were no longer afraid of him. They would
sometimes give him a bad time about giving him his
keys at the start of his shift.

They were just kidding, he didn't mind.

There were a great many keys on his ring, most
of them practically identical—he didn't rate a master.
Even after months on the job they still looked alike,
so he went through the trouble of color-coding them
with small round stickers.

Once he picked up his keys and all the stickers
had been removed. Another time all the stickers had
been switched around. There wasn't much point in
complaining—the keys went through a lot of hands
during the day—but Sloper had to wonder about
the guard who sat behind the console on Mondays
and Tuesdays, Dedlow or Ludlow, a big indolent kid,
almost as big as Sloper, rosy-cheeked, with a sparse
blonde mustache and a mouth full of small brown
stones. He did not like being asked for keys—it
would take him away from the monitors, especially
those looking out on the exterior entranceways and
alcoves, where street people frequently came to pee

or defecate. These locations were fitted with loud-speakers, and the kid would watch and wait for that singular relaxed moment critical to the act before barking into the microphone: "This is not a public restroom! Take your business elsewhere!" Some fled though they'd already gotten started, and some finished what they'd begun.

When asked for keys the kid would, with the elaborate discomfiture of the mortally inconvenienced, roll his chair back from the console to the key box behind the desk, groping inside with considerable difficulty and reluctance, looking only with his hand, his eyes always on the monitors, eventually returning with a set of keys, proffering them with renewed disinterest, and on the point of dropping them into your palm, suddenly retract them, saying, "Whups, wrong set. You want number 4," or "Sign the log first, fireball," or would withdraw them in increments, making you reach further and further in for them, saying, "How's that? Wrestling's fake? Huh, fireball? Get you in one of them holds, see how fake it is then." All the while never looking away from the screens.

By the time Sloper decided that maybe this wasn't kidding, that maybe he should say something about it, the kid was gone. Security had a terrific turnover.

Sloper kept his hard tile mopped, and he was good about glass. He squatted on his haunches in front of the lobby doors, head tilted back, and in this way could see every smudge and handprint. The cleaner was a pale green liquid in a plastic spray bottle that you refilled at the mixing center. Sloper used paper towels only—cloth smeared and left lint. He burned off a case a month. He didn't think it should be so hard to use the door handle, the panic bar, or the handplate, but he didn't take it personally that they didn't. Too, you had to figure how busy they were.

Aside from this commitment to clarity, Sloper left the detailing to the women. The edging, the deep dusting, kicking out. It was understood.

The glass cleaner went into one of numerous pouches on the yellow plastic apron strapped to his cart, along with the other spray bottles and cleaning supplies. If pouches were empty you could use them to hold burgers and sandwiches. If a burger or sandwich no longer had a wrapper you used a paper towel from another pouch on the yellow plastic apron. It was okay if a sandwich or burger was half-eaten. Potato salad from the deli in the lobby came in small plastic tubs that would also fit into the pouches, as would donuts, bagels, cookies, rice cakes, croissants, muffins.

People never finished their potato salad.

In the smallest yellow plastic pouch Sloper kept his only other diversion, a transparent plastic cube containing three silver balls of various diameter and three loose cups, correspondingly sized. He was usually unable to cup more than two of the balls without dislodging one or both, and it could be difficult to place just one.

The cart the yellow apron was strapped to was a gray Rubbermaid barrel screwed to a round pedestal with five casters, one of which rattled with bad bearings. When you trashed a floor, you dumped all the wastebaskets into the liner in your barrel. When the barrel was full, the Safety Committee asked, did you push it or pull it? It was a surprise visit. They asked Sloper nineteen other questions and then had him demonstrate the proper method of removing a full bag from the cart. Then he signed his name twice. You double-tied the bag and dropped it down a chute in the core of the building, all the way down to a dumpster in the first basement. Throughout the night you could hear the chutes booming distantly, like artillery. Sloper would periodically check the trash room to make sure a dumpster wasn't overloaded and backed up into a chute, that bags hadn't landed on the floor and burst. Doing so, he might hear a faint languorous beeping fade in, getting louder as the truck from the waste management company backed up to the garage door.

The trash was picked up every night after midnight. The guy who came in for the dumpsters said, "Howdy" and Sloper said, "Morning." When he left the guy said, "Have a good one" and Sloper said, "You bet." In the interval they rarely spoke, unless it was to discuss the possibility of a compactor, of which lately there'd been talk. They didn't always see each other, and neither called the other by name.

After the trash had been picked up, Sloper swept and mopped the trash room floor. He swept in slow circles, the pile of dirt and debris in the middle of the floor getting smaller and higher, and smaller, higher, as he spiraled in around it. He mopped in figure eights, changing the water once—he never put the dirt back on the floor. At the end of the night he put his vacuum sweeper in the empty Rubbermaid and pushed it into a closet. The sweeper's bumper was fitted with magnets for picking up loose paper clips, staples, tacks. If you didn't clear them off now and then, something could work its way under the spindle and jam the belt. The bag was supposed to be emptied every three nights but sometimes Sloper waited weeks. Sometimes his routine was interrupted by his supervisor or another janitor, who called on him to do the heavy lifting or plunge a shitty toilet, because of his apparent strength and because the building had no utility person. Sloper did not receive utility pay but this was how he got out of detailing, out of kicking out. It was understood.

The service preferred the janitors call it trash, not garbage, no matter what it smelled like.

The whole basement to himself. A refrigerator next to the furnace to keep beer in. A shower he used irregularly. A microwave and TV in his room.

The people on the second floor were not to use the basement. His mother wouldn't come down—the stairs killed her hips like crazy. Varicose veins bulged like fingers gripping her legs. He hadn't seen her in he didn't know how long. He didn't know how long it had been since he came home from the park on the river and saw all the shiny bits of paper scattered on the front steps, the lawn, the driveway. Some of the bits were larger than others and Sloper had glimpsed parts of bodies from his magazines. A small mob of kids frantically snatched them up, chasing the scraps the wind had, clutching them to their bodies as if to hide them under their skin. Then the magpies fluttered querulously in for what was left.

Once a month he would push a thick envelope under her kitchen door upstairs. Cash only. He was not to use the kitchen, he was to do the laundry. She sent it down the chute in a plastic bag, instructions written on an index card in the bag. She told him which stains had to be treated first. Sloper returned them folded or on hangers per her instructions.

From the windows over the washer and dryer you could see the side porch of the house next door. The wheelchair on the porch had lavender upholstery, pneumatic tires with mag rims, articulating legrests. The front casters reminded Sloper of baby carriage wheels. A stocky, serious-looking woman pushed the wheelchair, and you could tell she knew what she was about. When she came to a curb or some other obstruction she would lower her head and whisper, then place her foot on either of the step tubes jutting like exhaust pipes from the back of the frame—the way Sloper stepped on the axle of the hand truck when he moved recycling—before tilting the wheelchair back and then returning the front casters gently to the ground in a single unbroken motion. To do this you would need to be strong in the upper body, and Sloper saw her lifting weights on the little flagstone patio in the backyard. She ran for blocks clutching dumbbells, wearing a sweatsuit emblazoned with logos, the same logos Sloper saw on the polo shirt and baseball cap she wore. Sometimes headphones covered her ears.

Sloper's mother stomped on his head.

She rented out the floor above her and the tenants would get out of hand. Arguments or parties, it was hard to tell. She stomped on the floor, she yelled down the register that they were getting out of hand like crazy. Sloper didn't know what she expected of him. If he felt up to it he would yell back up that she should call the police, or call whoever it was, Virginia or Veronica, the relation, the aunt or cousin who took care of certain things. But she wouldn't do anything, wouldn't call anybody or start proceedings of any kind, either because they paid their rent on time, or because she was afraid of trouble, or of Virginia or Veronica, whoever it was.

The caregiver spooned food from a utility tray that slid into lock-tubes under the armrests. When not in use it rode behind the wheelchair next to the water bottle. She would adjust the angle of the back-rest with a pair of ratchet handles located beneath the handgrips. She used vinyl cleaner on the uphol-stery and waxed the chrome till it was engulfed in sunlight. She spun the wheels, checked the tire pres-sure, strummed the spokes like guitar strings. Oiled the center bolt in the crossbraces so they scissored smoothly together when the chair was folded.

Sloper watched her on the side porch as she drilled holes in the wooden footplates and attached heel and toe loops. She worked the little garden be-hind the patio. A ramp let out the back door there. A longer, more elaborate one switchbacked to the lawn in front. There was a van but it had no lift, and sometimes a white cloud rose from the hood when they pulled up.

A telescoping IV pole braced to the frame of the wheelchair. From the basement window Sloper saw the tip of it quiver past like an antenna. He guessed they were going to the park on the river—it wasn't far. He hadn't been there in he didn't know how long.

At night he saw someone's head float past the

window above the side porch. It drifted upward from left to right without bobbing. His mother stayed where she was, wouldn't take steps up or down.

Trespassers would get in the building—floor-walkers, in security parlance. Xeroxed warnings were posted in the copier rooms, some of which came from the security staffs of other buildings, where suspicious-looking strangers were seen on floors prior to discovered thefts, or were confronted by employees, providing hurried explanations or a mute opposing stare.

Someone had smeared shit on the restroom walls.

The posters gave a physical description. About 5'9", light-brown skin, short hair, blue windbreaker. He walked onto 10 with a vacuum sweeper. Sloper was trashing the floor. The man had said he was a replacement, he'd dropped the supervisor's name. Sloper didn't know anybody was sick. 10 was his floor, he said. He told the man with the vacuum sweeper he should go back down and check with the supervisor.

"Well alright then," the man said, very fast, almost impatient. He talked that way. After he left Sloper discovered the sweeper was his own.

A guard came up asking him if he'd seen a colored guy. Sloper said no—he didn't want to spend an hour filling out an incident report, black felt-tip only, didn't want them thinking he'd let someone onto the floor. Now Security made special rounds on 10, and too many people worked overtime as it was. There was Italian, but it was too risky.

A girl on 24 was nice to him. They were not always nice on 24, especially not after Christmas when they were preparing the Annual Statement. Employees worked late and offered to trade jobs with him, without smiling. Or they said nothing, just sat motionless at their computers while he emptied their trash, looking buried, sealed in. He'd seen a movie once. A U-boat stranded on the ocean floor, sweating out depth charges. The look on the faces of the crew, the same pressurized dread.

The IRS accountant kept his door locked, left

his wastebasket outside his door. Sloper asked the receptionist if he should just leave it there.

"No," she said. "Fill it with water and leave a crust of bread." He didn't get it but she smiled tightly and laughed through her teeth, a squeaky tremolo that reminded Sloper his steering belt was shot. His mother's steering belt. The receptionist returned to her desk. Tacked to the partition behind her was an old newspaper photo in which she stood on a stage in stockings and top hat, holding a baton. The caption named a dinner theater production. Another of her marching in a parade dressed like Uncle Sam. Next to that a dark cape and a shiny theatrical mask fringed in peacock feathers, under a small forked banner declaring ALL THE WORLD'S A STAGE! laser-printed in two colors.

Sloper always could never wait to get off the floor. The cubicle walls were too high and the passages between them too narrow—if you ran into him and his Rubbermaid it was a squeeze. The carpet always smelled new and suffocated every sound but the keyboards, a furtive patter that made Sloper think of roaches scuttling. For some reason he suffered chronic bouts of compulsive throat-clearing on 24, as if in preface to the great pronouncement of his life. He couldn't help it. The fluid rattled in his throat until he felt compelled to say something to somebody, hello or excuse me, which he said once, one of those, to a guy who was busily typing on his keyboard, who turned and smiled and replied in kind, typing all the while, and then turned back to the screen and stopped, a look of puzzlement on his face turning to disbelief, then something worse, saying "I don't believe I did that," and then repeating it, or variations thereof, over and over, moaning like someone with a bad tooth. Sloper could hear him till he was out in the elevator lobby. He wouldn't have taken it personally if the guy hadn't answered, or had grunted noncommittally without looking up, as they sometimes did.

A couple of times there were loud arguments. Some of the memos that tumbled out of the trash cans into his barrel got pretty salty for a bunch of bookkeepers, though Sloper wasn't usually much of a reader.

The girl who was nice to him on 24 smiled and

said hello. She told him how much she appreciated what he did. She had a regular voice and straight hair, but Sloper sometimes wondered a little about her, about if maybe she was passing for something she wasn't, if there was something in her blood that was darker than her skin. But of course you couldn't just ask, and he liked her thick muscular calves and watching them walk away from him when he knelt before the lobby doors. She worked late often, even when the Annual Statement was done. She kept a pair of sneakers under her desk. When she left she put on the sneakers and left her pumps under the desk. She'd go the ladies' room carrying a magazine called *The Progressive*.

Sloper never knew what to say to her. There were too many words to choose from. His mind would arrive at "good" and "cool" and his mouth would be unable to decide. It would come out "gool."

When she was gone he jerked off in her shoes and cleaned them out with germicidal foam. You could use it on anything but woodwork.

*   *   *

You had to remember where you put things. You could carry a cardboard box if someone was still on the floor. You could take a container out from under the desk you remembered and put it in the box. You wiped off the tray if you had to and used solvent if anything had gotten on the carpet. You carried the box onto the freight elevator like all the other boxes that were to be flattened and recycled. Sloper had a manual-override key. He could park the freight between floors. He would sit on the floor eating with the fork he kept on his cart, smelling his farts, maneuvering the cups and balls in the little plastic cube. He almost broke his tooth on a staple embedded in mashed potatoes.

Sometimes you couldn't wait for the microwave in the travel agency. You crossed your legs on the floor next to the trash can, alert to footfalls, the whisper of clothes, the jingling of keys. There were close calls. The rustle of paper in the fax machine was like hearing a ghost.

\*    \*    \*

Sloper's mother still packed her son a lunch. She'd send it down the chute and Sloper took it in case. If he didn't need one he saved it till he got home at night, napped through lunch in the freight or went outside. Otherwise he ate it in the cafeteria. Everyone sat grouped roughly according to nationality, each table a linguistic faction. Sloper sat alone between Russian and Ethiopian, his appearances too infrequent for him to have established a place with anyone else. Your American woman usually ate with her own kind at a table somewhere behind him, loudly or whispering, with their man problems and their kid problems, their potlucks and their aceydeucey. The only one decent-looking was also the loudest. Sloper wasn't sure of her name, or if her hair was really that color.

Most of the janitors wore their ID badges clipped to their breast pockets, and if they weren't looking at you their badges still were. Sloper's was clipped to his cart. He hadn't worn a badge that way since the city morgue, since Bernie and L.C. and Ahmed.

We the Four Horsemen, Ahmed would say. He'd picked it up watching wrestling on TV. They'd call each other nigger, and sometimes they'd call Sloper one, too. And Bernie's big laugh. He never wondered if it wasn't the memory he was more in love with, he only knew there was no one like that here. There was Bell, and once Bell made him turn over all the umbrellas he'd come early to take off Bell's floor. He didn't say stupid nigger then, not after the morgue; he hadn't thought it—at least, he didn't think he'd thought it.

Bell sat within bickering distance of the Hispanic table. You could tell he had a thing for the bathroom girl, the way he liked to argue with her and make her lisp her esses. Like the supervisor, she couldn't manage her vees, either. She had forty bathrooms a day to clean, which worked out to less than twelve minutes per bathroom, a quotient she was fond of repeating. These days she was fonder of reminding everyone they were working without a contract. Sloper heard her speak of gray areas, the need for clarified language in the new agreement—whatever that was about.

She reminded them what was happening in Silicon Valley.

Bell snorted. Once Bell had worked for Ford—Engine Plant No. 1—UAW days, but these were dog eat dog days. Bell was figuring on the floor crew, and then ultimately the window washers. There were waiting lists but those guys cleaned up.

"That's a play on words," he said. "What do you say?" he asked Kwang, who sat alone like Sloper but because his food smelled so bad. Kwang grinned gold teeth and said, "Hard work good."

Bell told him his lunch smelled like a female problem. The loud woman laughed louder than anybody. Sloper stole a glance at her, watched her laugh and roll the dice, wanting a new man, someone nice but not too nice. She'd done nice. Sloper would have liked her to know he could be that, he could straddle that line, but he didn't know the dialect. There was Vietnam and there was Mexico; Sloper was a language unto himself.

"If he was the last man on earth," she said about someone, "I'd break off a tree branch."

*     *     *

There were no cubicles on 18, just two long rows of computers. And the Bloomberg. The computers stayed on after everyone left—the receptionist, the office manager, the investment bankers. When you got there the lights were off and you saw within the flickering screens luminous green towers of numbers and statements, shifting, rising one line at a time with no top or bottom. About the only time you saw a blank screen in the building was in the basement, where monitors and keyboards sometimes ended up, consigned to a dumpster. Sloper took one home once, and now it sat blankly in his basement room. He'd heard that sometimes there wasn't all that much wrong with them. You could read up on it, or talk to someone.

Your investment baker didn't eat much, or they went out for lunch. All you ever found in their trash were orange peels and apple cores, wrapped in wax paper.

The Bloomberg displayed more than columns of figures. The Bloomberg had news and talking heads, anchors who were handsome and sculpted like the ones who did entertainment shows. Singapore was on the Bloomberg now, gleaming, prosperous, an Emerald City of skyscrapers and theme parks. It looked to Sloper like the place to live. No crime, no unemployment, public flogging for vandalism or blasting music—he figured he could go without chewing gum if he had to. That wasn't so much to ask.

Things were going up in flames in Singapore: TV sets, a Mercedes, even gold bars burning up like they were made of cardboard and papier-mâché. They were, the anchorman said. Part of a funeral ceremony, Buddhism or Confucius or something. Then the anchorwoman started talking about gold shares and they showed the real article being poured in molten form, then in bricks. Either way they had about the same glow to them.

The partner said it was time for a new paragraph. He was working late again. No one else in the firm ever did—even the associate had stayed after hours only once that Sloper could remember. The partner seemed like a nice guy but you couldn't go into his office to empty his trash or vacuum when he was dictating.

You couldn't make any noise.

"For the surviving issue of a deceased child comma," the partner said, "by right of representation comma—no, period. Period."

The firm was small but the kitchen had a sofa and a television, and sometimes Sloper used the microwave or sat on the sofa wiggling the little plastic cube, watching sitcoms with the sound off, but not if he heard the partner in his office, the click of the Dictaphone.

"I thought it was understood that I came to you as your friend and second cousin, not just as your lawyer, but if you insist then the total time consumed is one hour: sixty dollars, plus five if you care to add mileage." You would have to work around him then, go through the motions, and sometimes you had to come back later just to empty the trash.

Occasionally, though Sloper wasn't much of a reader, a piece of handwritten correspondence tumbling out of the wastebasket would end up in his hand.

"The agreement was that the garage door would be open and the children would come out when I honked. For the last year I have had to come to the door. Typically, you would communicate to me at the door or come to the car if the children had already come out. I am all in favor of communicating only in writing."

Sloper was not to touch the two hexagonal glass display cabinets at the front of the partner's office. They had black lacquered wood frames with handpainted floral patterns. He was especially not to touch the little soldiers behind the glass, the Highland regiment defending its compound against a horde of Zulus. They wore white colonial helmets and stiff red tunics with ugly plaid breeches, aimed rifles from behind tiny green crates. The tribesmen were tall and pretty, and though their spears and zebra-skin shields looked to be no match for the rifles, the fighting was at close quarters and they seemed on the verge of overrunning the compound.

The partner's collection was expanding, there was no more room in the glass cases—a squad of Union infantry marched rigidly across the coffee table in front of his couch. Black faces and thick pale lips. Their leader had light-beige skin and sat on a horse, facing gray cavalry in full charge. Plastic elephants harnessed to artillery with little brass chains, accompanied by bearded native foot soldiers wearing turbans, collecting dust. Everything was meticulously handpainted and Sloper wondered if the partner had done it himself or if he'd bought them that way. Once he heard him dictating a letter to the people who sold him the little soldiers.

Once he heard him on the phone with someone, asking someone, "Did you get on the diving board? The high or the low board? Was she with you?"

Asking, "Did you jump or dive? Did you do a cannonball? Can you?"

Except when Sloper walked by the office the partner was holding the framed picture of a child and not the phone. "I'll bet you did. Was she watching you? Hey, I can show you how to do one. I'll show you a half gainer and a can opener, too."

Sloper had heard that dust was nothing but dead skin.

She was either a vegetarian or watching her weight. In her trash can you would find a small tray with bits of fruit on a soggy piece of lettuce. A blueberry muffin that had been eaten down only to its paper cup. The muffin would fit into one of the small pockets on the yellow plastic apron.

The name on her nameplate had a hyphen in the middle. It repeated itself all over the walls, framed under glass, a series of certificates confirming her standing in a society of actuaries, her fluency in a number of electronic languages, her quality, her excellence, her achievement, her outstanding achievement and merit. She swung a golf club in a picture on her desk. A man presented a salmon. She and the man, a boy, and a girl sat in a gondola on a canal. Sloper looked at the girl and felt vaguely heartbroken again. In the wastebasket he found a pair of black stockings

like a consolation prize. There was no one else on 7.
He put one stocking over his head, his nose flattened
like a bank robber. The other mittened his hand. He
sat in her chair with his pants open and moved the
picture to the front of the desk. When he was ready,
he took the stocking off his head and slipped it on.
In the picture he drifted from the girl to the actuary.
After all they were her stockings, her musty emptiness
he'd slipped himself into.

He heard a key gnawing at the lobby doors.
Jerking at his zipper, Sloper caught himself in its
metal teeth. He clapped nylon over his mouth and
ducked under the desk. He pulled the chair in. Keys
jingled, coming closer, the carpet thumped with
somebody's approach. He'd left the light off, there
was only what came in off the floor, but his cart was
just inside the door. Through the gauzy dimness he
saw the office darken as the doorway filled. His face
throbbed against nylon.

He heard the bearings rattle as the casters rolled,
just a little, back and forth just a little.

When the guard had gone Sloper spent the

better part of an hour trying to finesse himself out of his predicament. He ended up finishing the shift with his workshirt untucked and hanging out over his middle. By the time he got home he was desperate enough to take hold and yank as hard as he'd been afraid to, leaving a small wad of uncircumcised flesh and black hose embedded in the metal teeth.

On his way back from the park he took the esplanade. He kept to the rail and walked slowly, stopping to stare at the river. The city's shattered reflection struggled to rebuild itself but the current wouldn't let it. As if it could become something else. From this turmoil a thin line emerged, nearly invisible, slanting tautly upward to a fishing rod leaning against the rail. The caregiver stood next to the fishing rod. Sloper looked away. How long had she been there? Behind her traffic on the esplanade moved in both directions, on bike, on skates, on foot walking and running. The river flowed only one way. Sloper waited for an opening.

The caregiver spoke.

You could see part of the wheelchair on the other side of her, and he wasn't sure if she'd spoken to him or to its occupant. He hadn't quite heard what she'd said. He didn't want to ask her to repeat herself, so to be on the safe side he asked if she'd had any luck.

"Just got here," she said. Sloper looked in the bucket at her feet and saw that it was empty.

"What are you fishing for?"

"Whatever's biting."

Eventually he thought up some more questions—about what she was using for bait, about what kind of fish inhabited the river.

At some point he noticed she would only answer in four words or less.

He asked her about the logos on the polo shirt and headband she was wearing.

"Promotional," she said. "Health care equipment."

Sloper wasn't much of a talker but found himself rising to the challenge. Wanted to see if he could get her to do it. He started out simple, working his way up to questions and observations that actually addressed several subjects at once, to which even the most general response would have to exceed four words. After two or three of these attempts he was conversationally depleted, while the caregiver was able to stay inbounds without missing a beat, almost never resorting to contraction.

Brevity was her second nature.

There was a beep.

The caregiver turned to the wheelchair. "Got a bite?" she asked. There were two more beeps. Sloper leaned over the rail to get a better look. Another line rose from the river and bent over the rail. It was tied to the wrist of the woman in the wheelchair. Her other hand rested on the black metal box in her lap.

"Cold?" the caregiver asked. The tendons in the woman's hand flexed and a small red light on the black box flashed twice. Sloper heard two more beeps. It reminded him of something. The woman had a sweater over her shoulders and she wore dark glasses. The wheel locks high on the sides of the chair were pulled to.

"Got it," the caregiver said, facing forward again.

Sloper asked, "Don't they have those computers that can talk for you?"

"Bend-over city," the caregiver said. The woman in the wheelchair beeped twice.

"Her fingers can't letterboard." Two beeps.

The caregiver sighed. "She prefers this."

"Huh."

"It narrows things down."

"So how do you talk?"

"You start broadly."

"Huh."

"You'd be surprised." The woman in the wheel-chair beeped once and they both looked to see if she had a bite. Her head never moved. Behind her dark glasses you couldn't see if she could see you looking at her and was looking back at you. There was gray in her hair but you couldn't tell how old she was. The skin on her cheeks and on the backs of her hands was taut and shiny in patches, but you couldn't tell. The wind rose. Her skirt blossomed and showed Sloper a diaper. On the long green lawn beyond the esplanade, he saw a dog bite a Frisbee in midair. Kids screamed around the fountain near the street. A war memorial, dead soldiers remembered in black stone. The grass covered with blankets. People covered the blankets and were sometimes covered with other people.

"She loves it," the caregiver said. Sloper looked at her but there was nothing else. She seemed to be smiling.

The woman in the wheelchair beeped. She began appending beeps to nearly everything the caregiver said. It definitely made Sloper think of something. The caregiver would explain these interjections, which explanations were sometimes subject to further editorial beeping. Still, she only used four words at a time. Or less. Sloper thought about trying it himself.

Then the caregiver said, "So, neighbor, do you come here often?"

If the trash in one of the dumpsters was piled so high it was plugging the chute, you had to relieve the excess. If you didn't feel like climbing into the dumpster and taking it off the top, you could use the sliding door in the front of the dumpster and reach through an opening the size of a car window.

Sloper opened the door and pulled out a bag. The plastic ripped and garbage spilled onto the floor. As if to punish him for this, somebody hit him in the face. He dropped the bag and stepped back, his vision blurred. When he could see he saw a pale arm hanging out of the square opening, not hitting him anymore or doing anything else.

He stopped swallowing blood and went back to the arm. It showed almost to the shoulder and was bare, a woman's arm. Sloper's face still felt where it had been struck. He pulled another bag from inside the dumpster and saw to the collarbone. Her face was as pale as her arm and her eyes were open. Her head was upside-down, which was why it took Sloper a while to recognize the girl from 24 who spoke to him. She had marks on her neck. She was paler than usual.

His nose started bleeding again.

He paced the trash-room floor with a rag pressed to his face, shaking the plastic cube. The best he could do was one ball in one cup.

\*    \*    \*

Reaching through the square opening, he pulled bags off her shoulders and chest. So far she was still naked. Because of the angle at which she lay, her breasts had rolled back on her chest almost to her throat. They were bigger than he'd thought.

The building had leftover carpeting. Tile, strips, and rolls, stacked in the corner next to the basement utility room. Contractors just left it. The building had let it be known that anyone could help themselves.

Sloper walked back to the trash-room with the biggest roll he could find under his arm. He passed a closed-circuit camera oscillating on its perch at the top of a support column. Not that it mattered who was watching the monitors—he was allowed to do what he was doing.

His gloves were made of thick suede with metal beads sewn into the palms for grip. Still, she gave him a bad time. She lay at an angle and there was weight on her—the whole building, it seemed. Her arms were no help. Her arms brought him nothing but trouble. One was looser than the other and could swing all the way back at the shoulder. It would have been easier if they both could have. He tried pulling her by the hair but he didn't want to break her neck if he didn't have to.

You could smell it through the rank sweetness of the dumpster. He'd have to clean her.

He climbed up into the dumpster and started throwing trash into the one alongside. Somebody had dumped a wooden pallet. Contractors, probably. That would do it every time.

Something came rumbling down the chute. There was still plenty of time before the truck came.

His mother's wagon was parked in the third basement. Sloper drove it up the spiraling ramp and backed up to the trash room doors. He opened the doors and then backed the wagon halfway into the trash room.

He'd left her between the last dumpster and the back wall. He'd rolled her up in the carpet and pinched the ends like an outsize burrito. Dragging her out he thought he heard something in the basement. He listened and decided he was wrong. It was hard scooping her up and standing, not really knowing where the center was, and the carpet had its own weight. He got to the back of the wagon and he'd forgotten to pop the tailgate. He heard again what he thought he hadn't, something scraping the basement floor, echoing. To pop the tailgate you had to push a button inside the glove compartment. He practically had to just drop her under the back wheels.

Sloper squeezed past the side of the car. A man wearing a hardhat dragged a pallet toward him and said, "Hey." Sloper stood next to the passenger door.

"Hey," the man said. He wore pale blue overalls that looked like they were made of paper. "You're holding up progress."

Sloper said nothing.

"You want lung cancer?"

Sloper said no.

"Well then, how about it? We're scraping that

shit off as fast as we can but it's all over everything. Floor, pipes, you name it. So tiny you can't see it but we're breathing it as we speak, trust me. Fifteen, twenty years later you're reaching down you own throat to scratch that itch. Hawking up bits of lung like there's no tomorrow—all because of a station wagon. Come on, I'm burning up in this spacesuit."

Sloper looked at the pallet. "I can throw it away."

"The union would kill me." The man winked.

"Could you just leave it?" Sloper opened the door and reached for the glove compartment. "I just have to get something."

"What?"

"Nothing."

"Something. Nothing." The man leaned on the edge of the pallet like it was a fence. "Nobody sweats like that over nothing."

Sloper pressed the button. Sometimes it stuck. "Carpet."

"Yeah? Bet you there's cancer in it."

"Huh," Sloper said.

"Hey." The man glared. "How do you rate?"

"Rate what?"

"They wouldn't let me leave my Jimmy down here. Somebody put a big sticker on the windshield right in front of my face: Don't-Park-Here-You-Asshole. Signed, Adolf Hitler. I practically had to chisel it off."

"Huh."

"Guard's probably on the way as we speak." He looked up and to the side where the camera was, waving an arm. "Hey, down here. Wake up." He raised a middle finger. "That oughta do it. Maybe they'll send down whatshername, with the long legs? Get me in a chokehold with em, I'll have to lick my way out. Don't you love a girl in uniform?"

Sloper said nothing.

"They're not paying me to stand here smalltalking, you know. You know what the prevailing wage is for scraping cancer?"

"You could just leave that there."

The man gripped the pallet and twisted back. "Maybe I can make it from here." He winked. "How much says I won't scratch your wagon from here?"

"I'll do it," Sloper said.

"Scrape, scrape," the man said.

Sloper lived across the river from the city center. The sidewalks downtown were pretty much rolled up by the time he got off work, but The Native Son was never quite closed when he drove past. People seemed reluctant to leave, and once in a while a police car was parked out front with its lights flashing. It looked like the kind of place Bernie would have liked. Sloper thought about stopping there some time for last call if he could get up the nerve. He'd seen a few white people. He thought it might help to affect a limp—people were less likely to bother you then. Maybe even Bell would be there.

Near the bridge that would take him across the river a storefront promised ADULT ENTERTAIN-MENT. Videos, gadgets, you could talk to live girls. You couldn't see inside, all the glass was blacked out. Open twenty-four hours, according to the neon.

Sloper had been inside once. There were two

live girls. They sat outside their booths sizing up customers. The younger one had breast implants and wouldn't give him the time of day. The dumpy one told him thirty dollars. He said he'd think about it. When he was checking out the playlist for the video booths, he noticed her standing next to him.

"Okay," she said. "Twenty dollars for a masturbation show." He almost asked her who was supposed to masturbate. She started following him around the store. By the time she was down to ten bucks, she'd scared him out the door. He was supposed to be the desperate one.

Somebody in the firm left a note about the cabinet under the kitchen sink. Nobody was around. Sloper got on his hands and knees and pulled everything out of the cabinet. He picked up the trash and swept out the coffee grounds under the drain with a foxtail. The floor and back wall were badly stained and needed scrubbing. Sloper got a sponge from his cart and a bottle of #11, the heavy-duty stuff. He got back on his knees and stuck his head and shoulders into the cabinet under the sink.

Nobody was around till the partner said, "Not a wink."

Sloper banged his head on the sink trap. "Don't mind me," the partner said. "I'll be right out of your way. Let me just get things going here."

Sloper rubbed his head with the sponged hand. He heard a coffee pot ring.

"Just let me get in your way here for a second," the partner said. The cabinet darkened. Sloper twisted his head back and saw the partner's feet planted on either side of his legs. He didn't have any shoes on. Water ran, the underbelly of the sink thrummed over his head. The trap shook and bits of rust powdered off the drainpipe. Sloper twisted a knuckle in his eye.

"Stomach has a mind of its own. Stomach said: No sleep for us tonight, coffee for you and me. We've got a probate to push. Gotta get going on the garnishees.

"I said, You're the boss," the partner said. Sloper sprayed #11 on the back wall. It glowed ominously like vitamin-rich piss, and though they gave it a cloying lemony fragrance it was in fact strong enough to strip paint. He figured it wouldn't matter under here.

The faucet was off. The feet went away. Sloper realized he didn't have his mask. He heard the partner saying how good it smelled. "Deep cleaning, huh? I'll bet you guys sleep easy. You know what Dad said? About trash? Dimestore philosopher, said we should envy it. Said trash was free to be itself, finally innocent of any human purpose." Water gushed into the reservoir of the coffeemaker. "Know what Dad's Dad did? Walked. Back then they still delivered on foot. You could have your thoughts and all the exercise you'd need. In the winter people left hot rum in the mailbox. "

"You call that a job?" the partner said. "He loved to walk, lived till he was ninety-three."

"Do you like to walk?"

Sloper started scrubbing the wall so he wouldn't have to answer. Figured it didn't matter anyway. The partner said, "All they have to do is say something, just make a monthly agreement, and we'll walk away. Just send something, we won't even ask for the whole judgment... Why don't they answer? It's nothing personal."

The coffeemaker made a noise.

"I've got to," the partner said.

"I can't," he said.

"I just," he said.

"If only."

Sloper felt queasy. His mask was in a pocket of the yellow plastic apron on his cart. He rubbed in short fast strokes, making a harsh, industrious sound. A sound that meant business.

"Looks great in here. It really does." The partner's voice was going away. The coffee maker gurgled. "Don't worry about me. I'll clean up after myself."

When the doors opened on 15 a cool wind pushed into the elevator. The investment bankers were gone. They'd taken their computers and all their furniture. The carpet had been pulled up. There were wheelbarrows and ladders everywhere. Across the floor, part of a wall was missing—just slender metal studs and a fifteen-story drop in the night. Dusty sheets of plastic hung rustling from the ceiling. A welding torch flared, sparks fell.

Sloper stood there with his hand truck waiting for the doors to close. One of the hardhats grinned. "Hey, you're letting in a draft."

No one ever told him anything.

He smelled refrigerator. He'd taken the racks out, put his beer on the door shelves, ate frozen dinners. He kept it on high and kept an eye on the thermometer—you didn't want it getting below thirty-five.

The women next door were gone. The caregiver said something about a cabin and better fishing. They'd taken the van.

He rolled onto his side and turned her over with him, spooning her against him so he could hold her front. She wouldn't warm up but he liked how she looked in the TV glow, bluish, a vampire hungry for his heat. He liked holding her. He liked one skin touching another skin, and the third thing they made. He squeezed her and she farted on him. He closed her eyes again. Maybe an electric blanket.

With his finger in a washcloth he'd scraped out her mouth, nose and ears. That was where they laid their eggs. He'd learned it at the morgue.

The ceiling thumped. The vents delivered his mother's complaints—the people upstairs. They wouldn't have it in Singapore.

The elevators in the lobby wouldn't go to the top floor. You had to take a shuttle from the floor below, and you needed a key. Most of the employees had been there once, on the day of their orientation, and had never been back. Years would pass, and when you retired the president came down and shook your hand—there was no need to go upstairs again.

Sloper didn't work for the building, the service was under contract. He rode the shuttle every night, holding his rake like a farmhand. He got there after the floor had been cleaned, and no one there ever worked late. The curtains were drawn by electric motor. The desktops were sparsely, geometrically arranged, and without clutter, as if they had hardly anything to do all day, but Sloper knew of course this wasn't the case. Not even liners in the trash cans, and nothing to eat.

The rake had a long handle and a wide dustless brush with long, thick bristles. When you were done you had to pluck loose fibers out of the bristles like hair out of a hairbrush. The carpet was blue-gray, deep pile, so thick you felt it pushing back with each step. Sloper raked with his shoes off for better purchase. When you took the footprints out in the offices you had to work around the furniture. In the open areas you worked in long single strokes, wall to wall, and when you reached a wall you started back in the opposite direction so that the grain of the pile swept both ways and the footprints disappeared in stripes, two shades of absence.

The previous regime of executives, Sloper had heard, did not approve of stripes, and Sloper's predecessor had had to rake the carpet in one direction only, leaving a uniform expanse like a calm sea. It would take three hours. And they'd had different taste in art, favoring the cold, modern stuff, incomprehensible except in that it was as ruthlessly symmetrical as the floor itself. With the new outfit a more traditional sensibility presided. Historical. A bare-chested Indian whipping a herd of wild horses over a jagged escarpment. "Red Man's Gold," the sculptor declared. In the reception area a bulky squaw tended a pot hanging from a rough tripod. A tepee rose behind her out of the snow, in the foreground a frozen creek. A mountain man approached holding a rifle, leading his horse by the bridle. The frame was a rough-hewn rectangle of wood, chipped and scarred, that looked to have survived the era it now enclosed. The president preferred landscapes.

It was bright and peaceful up there. You heard only the movement of air from the convectors, an occasional fax, noise from the street. Sloper worked in sections, turning out lights as he went. Even the street sounds sounded different as the footprints vanished—ugly but pure.

Somebody had to do it.

If you left a light on you had to backtrack over the area you'd raked to turn it off, then take out the footprints you'd left backtracking. Sometimes Sloper would see a ficus leaf fall onto a blankness he'd just made, and he would debate over doubling back to pick it up. The guards who made rounds after he finished were instructed to walk along the edges of the floor, and they almost always did.

You didn't have to rake the boardroom if it hadn't been used. The door would be locked to let you know, and you knew that inside the curtains were drawn, that the long table was covered with a black vinyl slipcover, that on the wall above a sideboard there hung three portraits: the founder, the first president, and the first chairman of the board, with their cravats, their timepieces and burnsides, their antiquated expressions still hanging there in that dark.

It was as high as Sloper could go. A short flight of stairs led from the fire exit up to a roof access door, but that was a key Sloper didn't have. Security did, and at night on the Fourth of July the guards treated themselves to the fireworks over the river.

The building was smokefree. If you smoked you took your breaks outside, on the plaza that surrounded the building at street level. Sloper didn't smoke but sometimes he would break outside, sitting on a bench with his little plastic game, or walking slowly around the building, passing smoky clusters of conversation.

"She doesn't have a car, they're not even sure she left the building."

"They know more than they say."

It was light outside or it was dark, depending on the time of year. In the late time of year the light was sharp and low-angle, harsh as an interrogation.

"You do the floor every night?"

"Was she there when you were?"

There were people on the plaza who didn't belong there. Security tolerated them unless they panhandled or skateboarded. Or went to the bathroom. Sometimes they asked if it was you who needed anything. Sloper shook his head or just walked away.

The occasional diversion of an arrest. Concrete tables with chessboards painted on the surfaces. Sloper stood among a small crowd, watching a game. A man came along with a shopping bag and offered him a sandwich. Sloper declined—he was not a street person. When he saw that it was egg salad he had second thoughts. Afterwards he made a point of hanging around the chess games when he was outside, but he kept missing the sandwich man.

Bruising was a problem. When she crouched in the fridge her buttocks turned purple like overripe fruit. Sloper tried rotating her, turning her on her head. Her breasts filled with blood. Her collarbone snapped.

He found an old washtub in the garage. He was going to bring home a mop bucket from work but the washtub was better. He laid her on her back on his bed, her head hanging off the footboard, put pillows under her legs and buttocks. A vein or an artery, he couldn't remember which. He wasn't sure which side so he opened them both, turned on the late late news and opened a beer.

There was nothing else on. Down here all you got were three snowy channels, sometimes four. It came out black and lumpy. He heard it spattering in the tub and got another beer.

Afterwards it was the inner thigh, he remembered, but it was hard to find exactly where and he nicked her up pretty good before it came. He kept forgetting it wouldn't heal—he could always spackle it with something, or maybe it wouldn't matter. He stood behind her in the shower, his arms under her armpits and clasped across her chest, hardening against her. She bled blackly on him and the water washed it off. He came quickly on her and the water washed it away. He lifted her, made her jump, trying to get it all out. It was a long night. The water cooled. He dozed, standing there with her. You couldn't expect to get every drop.

You could see the tracery of blue veins that networked her body just under the skin. Frozen, electric.

The women next door returned.

Another building was going up across the street. It was taller than the one Sloper worked in but right now it was just a skeleton with floor slabs. Tonight it was higher than the moon, you could see the moon right in its middle. They kept the working lights on at night after the construction workers left, blue and deep amber. The stairs were in, you could see them zigging and zagging all the way up and down. Someone was walking down the stairs, all the way from the top to the bottom, from the blue to the amber. Sloper stood at the windows on 10 and watched him every step of the way. He took a step to the side and made whoever it was walk down the moon. He wondered if it felt like anything. It would only have been better if whoever it was was going up.

"I will cease practicing law," the partner said, "some time before the first of next year." He never went home anymore. His door was closed. He left his wastebasket out in the hall.

"I am terminating my practice before the end of the year," he said. There was a sign on his door.

"If not complain," the supervisor said, "I'm don't worry."

"Based on your agreement with Ford Motor Company comma, you were to make monthly payments of $100.00." His voice boomed through the door. "Our records show that you are presently in arrears up to your ears, dipshit."

"I must advise you that I am closing down my practice of law before the new year. I would not sell a client's name period."

He said, "I do this as a matter of courtesy."

Sloper thought of the little soldiers in the partner's office, collecting dust. Skin.

"I am in the process of shutting down," the partner said. "I do not sell my clients."

"I will not continue to practice," he said.

"I am not renewing my license."

"I am going fishing," the partner said. "Back to the lake before it was a river. The mountains were still far away back then. Dad taught me how, and when I was old enough he let me go alone. Just me and a dozen nightcrawlers, my lantern, my spinning rod. We had our reasons, we had our favorite spot. Just a ragged patch of shoreline behind the old terminal comma busted concrete slabs and barbed wire. Rats, railroad tracks, but I was not ashamed, I know where

I come from. I caught slender yellow fish with fierce vertical markings.

"Drunk with a shotgun full of rocksalt chased me off. Told me the bulldozers were coming, the fences, the Yacht Club. The goddamn mountains. Chased me onto the breakwall north of the power plant. The hell with his mother's name, he did me a favor. I caught broad white fish with horizontal stripes, fish with thick hides and no scales. Never said I was a pro like Dad, I just still-fished the bottom but I always ate what I caught, even when they said you shouldn't. I wasn't the only one, but only at night, the lonely pockets of light we'd cast from, each one at such a remove from the others no one would risk the intervening darkness, the treachery it obscured, unless they wanted something that bad. They taught me to smoke and drink but I always kept those gleaming eyelets in the corner of my eye for the twitch of life, just a foot or so of line visible off the tip of the rod. Like we'd cast into night itself. There were men who'd waited that way half a lifetime.

"Ore freighters drifting on the edge of sight like

floating constellations, and always that sound, that song, white noise of decay. The treachery it obscures new paragraph.

"You get tired of waiting. Things get out of hand. Fish land with pink puckered sores like mouths riddling their scales. Twelve-year-old kids prowl the waterfront in shiny booming muscle cars, barely seeing over the wheel. Dad got rolled, lashed with his own rod and thrown in the water. They punished him every time he tried to swim home. He was all washed up. Long welts, pink bloated flesh, you know that story.

"Things get out of hand. They come in numbers to the rocks, tribes of them, form lairs in the cave spaces under the breakwall and wait for dark. Bad-luck fishermen caught from behind, dragged down into the spidery hollows, better-tasting than rats, fresh bait and brand new tackle untouched, untended rod propped like an antenna, quivering and bending with bite, no hand now to set the hook, just the sudden slack of line as the fish throws the bait or calls it quits, swims in to relieve its pain. Sorry Charlie, you were chosen but you were not there. You have not returned my calls.

I must say this is a shabby way to treat a colleague who has sent you some business, and despite what the realtor and title company say, your client's actions indicate to me that she has no intention whatsoever of purchasing the property despite having signed a binding contract.

"In plain English: by defaulting you forfeit the signing fee. It is ridiculous to think otherwise. Awaiting your reply,

Two steps led up to the fire door in the back of the trash room. On the other side a steep ramp rose from the parking garage to the street. Sloper left the door unlocked for the guy who drove the garbage truck. When he came back down to the trash room after the truck was gone, a man was sitting on the steps taking off his shoes and socks.

"Who are you?" Sloper asked.

"Who the wind blew in," the man said. "How's it going?"

"Okay," Sloper said. "But—" The man looked at him. He had both shoes off and one sock.

"What are you doing here?"

"I don't want any trouble," the man said.

"Me neither." Sloper made a face and stepped back.

"Sorry about that. If you let me dry these off," the man said, "I'll be gone in an hour. Two hours tops."

"I leave at two."

"An hour, then. On my mother's stone."

"I don't know." Sloper waited. "The guard might've seen you—there's a camera over the door."

"He'da been down here by now."

"I don't know."

"If you want me to leave, I'll go."

Sloper didn't say anything. He took the plastic cube out of his pocket and turned it without trying to accomplish anything. The man interpreted this gesture favorably and hung his socks over a pipe. He sat down. "Appreciate it." Sloper didn't answer. "Those doors lock on both sides?"

"Why?"

"If you got work to do you could lock me in. I'll go the way I came." He tapped an empty dumpster with his knuckle and made it ring.

"Maybe," Sloper said. "They're not really supposed to be, but."

The man had marks on his face, sores or welts. A growth in his neck. It bobbed when he spoke like a second Adam's apple. He asked Sloper if he had any spare change.

"No."

"Cans? Bottles?"

"They're not mine to give," Sloper said. "We pool em. Have a pizza party."

The man nodded, looking at the plastic cube. A thick chain looped around his shoulder, slanting across his chest. A padlock hung from it. He noticed Sloper staring. "My lugger," he said. "Strictly for self-defense. Can I see what you have there?" Sloper looked at him. "I'll give it right back."

Sloper tossed the cube over. "What's in the coop?" the man asked. He meant the enclosure in the opposite corner. Dusty, tarp-covered shapes behind a chain-link gate.

"Just old equipment, I think."

"They use it?"

"Why?"

The man turned the cube. "Thought maybe we could make an arrangement."

"I don't have a key." Sloper watched. "Can't you get in a shelter?"

"I guess I'd better. Now ask me why I don't work."

"You look able enough to me."

"I am in some ways."

"We're hiring."

"I'm holding out for a flat tax." The man held the cube still and grunted. "I'm not meaning to be a smartass. You need an address to get a job. You need a job to get an address. The chicken-and-egg routine."

"Huh." Sloper might have said there had to be more to it than that but he had work to do. And that smell. He moved. "I'm locking you in. You need to be gone in an hour."

"Thanks, partner." The man tossed the cube back. If he'd solved it, Sloper would never know.

"Partner?" Sloper stopped closing the doors.

"The egg," the man said. He smiled. "The egg that hatched the chicken that laid it."

He laughed. The laugh brought something else up and he spat it on the floor. Something shiny.

Sloper dialed a 9. His mother's phone was old. He was trying to put his story together. He dialed a 1. Something came apart and he hung up.

His story was to be in every way true. It started with him opening the basement door and switching on the light. Every time he came back around to the beginning it would start that way. Then he realized what wasn't quite right about it—the basement light had already been on—and he had to start the start of his story all over again.

Little things like that would make him disconnect, because once you dialed that third number that was it, they were in it and so were you, with them. They would insist on a story and then try to become part of it. This much he knew. The trick was to come up with a story no one else could find a way into.

He dialed a 9.

He started for a change in the middle. The fuse box. The open panel and the spent fuse on top of the dryer were right in the middle of his story. Then he went back to the first part where she was on the basement floor and he didn't move her because you weren't supposed to in a case like that, you might make things worse, and besides, the way her eyes were open. But you never knew if someone was beyond medical attention or not, and in his story that was why he got the pillow, it was the least he could do just in case. It was the truth.

It was a true story.

It had everything but the kitchen sink. And the refrigerator. The open refrigerator door was not in it. He'd meant to get a padlock, hadn't meant for her to see.

Her eyes still open with it.

Her heart still stopped with it.

He dialed a 1.

Before the last number was the story before the beginning. He put her hips there, and the stairs, and her heart. The stairs killed her hips like crazy, her hips killed her heart. Not to mention her veins. Not to mention the people upstairs, how good they were at getting out of hand, how they stressed and upset her. They were out of hand over his head right now as he sat there, holding the phone. Unless they were another story. You could put them in anyway. You could just mention them and trail off, leave a silence, make room.

But not for her. There was only room for her in the refrigerator. He didn't have to think about what she would do to it, his story. He wanted it to have an end. She would be the wrong one, or only another beginning. It depended.

The aunt took care of things. No one knew exactly who she was. They couldn't agree on which side of the family she belonged, whether her name was Virginia or Veronica, whether she actually was an aunt and not a cousin, or second cousin, or just some friend of the family on whom the status of honorary relation had been conferred. Sloper wasn't

sure either. Though you would only see her once in a
great while, during times of crisis, she would behave
in a completely familiar manner, warmhanded and
name-knowing, as if she took mutual recognition
for granted. By tacit agreement she was allowed to
take charge.

Deaths in the family were a specialty—she was
capable of expressing genuine grief on the one hand,
while shrewdly disposing practical affairs with the
other. A form of coordination. The funeral director suggested that if the body wasn't burned within
twenty-four hours, it should be embalmed. But the
aunt had done some shopping, the remains could be
refrigerated. A small service then, in the crematory
chapel, for what family there was. The casket closed
and rented for the service only—you burned it, you
bought it. When it sank beneath the chapel floor,
the aunt went down into the anteroom and made
sure Sloper's mother was transferred into a cardboard
container before going into the retort. Powder, she
told the funeral director unequivocally, not a bit of
bone. Mourning efficiently the whole while.

There was no reception. When Sloper got home an envelope with a brief note in it had been shoved under the door. He went straight to the refrigerator. There was getting to be a grayness about her if you looked closely, but that was okay, his eye was out for green. Green was bad news. It started in the belly and worked its way out. Sloper thought about the fake suntan you could buy in a bottle.

The next day he put on the same suit he'd worn to the service and rang the bell next door. The caregiver was dressed in somber, consoling colors, unadorned with advertising. The woman in the wheelchair wore a black armband. Sloper was prepared for uncomfortable preliminaries—his life was an awkward silence—but dinner was ready. Broiled fish the caregiver had caught herself. Baked potato, rolls, salad. The butter was unsalted but there was beer. Sloper had another helping. He liked ketchup with his fish but there was none at the table and Sloper wasn't good at asking.

They took turns glancing at each other. The woman in the wheelchair did not eat. Her hands remained on the black box in her lap. At intervals the caregiver inserted the tip of a long flexible straw in her mouth, and she would draw liquid from a lidded plastic container. The caregiver watched Sloper watching and said, "She's had her mush." The woman in the wheelchair beeped once. Sloper, beer in his mouth, expelled air through his nose.

"She thinks I'm funny," the caregiver said, and there was a beep. Once again Sloper was reminded of something. The caregiver looked up and said, "Am I forgetting anything?"

The woman in the wheelchair beeped once.

"The zinfandel?" There were two beeps and then the caregiver remembered. She straightened and turned to Sloper and offered formal condolences like another course. "If there's anything we can do for you," she concluded, "anything at all at this time."

Sloper thought and mumbled the word ketchup. The woman in the wheelchair beeped once.

The caregiver appeared to smile and rose to clear her place. "I'll bring some on the way back," she said. The woman in the wheelchair beeped twice. "I'll be just a second. I'm sure he doesn't mind." There were two more beeps.

The caregiver sighed and straightened. "You're right. What was I thinking."

While she was gone Sloper asked the woman in the wheelchair if they were sisters. She beeped twice. She beeped twice several times. Sloper smiled cautiously.

"I heard that," the caregiver called from the kitchen. Sloper remembered then. It came to him.

"Star Trek," he said. The woman in the wheelchair blinked and looked her eyes at him. "You remind me of something on Star Trek."

She did not beep.

"The pilot episode," Sloper said. "Commander Pike?" he said. "Antimatter... there was this explosion..." A baffleplate had given. The commander ruinously injured, completely paralyzed, confined to a wheeled contraption from which he can communicate only by means of beeps and flashing lights.

Sloper said, "I thought maybe that was where you got the idea." The woman in the wheelchair did not beep. The caregiver hadn't returned. "You didn't get the idea from there?"

The woman in the wheelchair beeped once. Sloper wasn't sure if this meant yes, she did get it from there, or yes, she didn't. "Do you want to talk about something else?" he asked finally.

She beeped once.

"What do you want to talk about?"

The caregiver returned with Sloper's ketchup. "Maybe she'd like to hear about you." She turned. "Ready for the zinfandel?" The woman in the wheelchair beeped before the caregiver was finished asking.

"Red or white?"

There was a silence. "Just joking," the caregiver said defensively. She gently detached the cup from its straw. "Conversation makes her mouth dry."

"Me," Sloper said to the woman in the wheelchair.

The woman in the wheelchair beeped once.

He waited. "My job?"

She beeped again.

"My job."

The woman in the wheelchair was silent while Sloper talked about his job.

"My mother?"

She beeped.

"The Olds?"

She beeped and flashed.

"The Olds needs a belt," Sloper said.

"The house?"

The woman in the wheelchair beeped.

"What about the house?"

The caregiver stood there. "Maybe she'd like to know if you're going to stay there." The woman in the wheelchair was silent again, and the caregiver looked as if she'd been reproached.

"Just trying to help," she said. She inserted the straw into the lid of the cup. The woman in the wheelchair took a long pull from her end, then pushed it out with the tip of her tongue. "We have partial use, don't we?"

"It's a nice house," Sloper said. "But it's not

paid for. My aunt's taking over the payments." He pronounced it ahnt. "Or something." He shook his head and shrugged simultaneously. He did that sometimes. "I'll be staying there, I guess. Is there any more beer?"

"The people upstairs," the caregiver said. The woman in the wheelchair beeped twice. The caregiver winced.

Sloper looked at each of them. "What about them?"

The woman in the wheelchair beeped twice.

"Nothing. None of our business," the caregiver said. "Maybe you'd like to watch a movie with us some time."

The woman in the wheelchair beeped once. With her tongue she pulled the straw back into her mouth. The caregiver went to the kitchen.

Contractors could use the freight to haul equipment—the building okayed it. Sloper opened the doors on 15. The floor looked almost finished. There were only three drywallers there, two men and a woman, and they got on the elevator empty-handed. He'd heard the floor had already been leased.

The woman reminded Sloper of a country singer. The older, meaner-looking guy looked at him appraisingly. They were going to the parking garage.

"Linebacker," one of them said.

"Tight end."

"Nose tackle."

"Hell," the older guy said, "he's not that big."

"Well?" the nicer guy said to Sloper.

"Ignore them," the woman said. Sloper didn't know what to say—he wasn't interested in sports.

"We need laborers," the nicer guy said. "Across the street. Feel like making some real money for a change?"

"Doing a man's work for a change?"

Sloper looked at the woman. They were all watching him so he felt he should say something. "Who's moving in?" he asked her.

"How's that?" the younger guy said.

"Watch it," the meaner guy said. "That's mine.

Won her in a pool game."

"Shut up," the woman said. "He wants to know who's moving in."

A thickness. It started in his belly and spread to every joint. He was hot all over, his skull throbbed. Gas seeped languidly out of him, so dense it oozed. So noxious it seemed barely human.

He took the elevator up and felt weaker on each floor—might as well have taken the stairs. He could barely push the hand truck. One of the accountants on 24 saw his pallid face, watched him struggle with the recycling, and asked if he was okay. She fled with her hand over her nose. Sloper barely noticed.

He sat on the toilet. The thickness was a big square shape with sharp edges, inside him but bigger than him, and it couldn't get out. It worked its way down in waves, down to his lower belly where the knife-pain was worst, and then suddenly faded, as if it had found some bodily exit unknown to him. Then it started all over.

Sloper knelt before the bowl and tried to throw

up. His stomach contracted. His belly touched his spine, his ribs were breaking. He belched and tasted the tuna melt he'd found on 5. He'd microwaved it to melt the cheese. It hadn't tasted wrong, but then it probably didn't have to.

Nobody was in the cafeteria. You weren't supposed to be there between breaks. Sloper collapsed into a chair and felt his forehead burning his arm. His shirt was soaked. He did not want to go home sick, he did not want to try to explain to his supervisor. He didn't think he could drive. He got to his feet with great effort and belched again.

There were plastic bags in a cupboard under the condiments and utensils. He nested three small bags and filled them under the ice machine. The air was getting thicker. He fought his way through it to the freight elevator and parked it between floors. He lay down in the dark, pressing the bag to his forehead, his belly.

His head filled with sound. Or was it the elevator?

He fell out of bed in his mother's room. Somebody had taken away her windows and covered him with stickers. Like the stickers on bananas, but smaller than the ones last year. Whoever had done it must have known he had to be somewhere, at an interview or appointment. The stickers were round and different colors, hard to get your nails under.

When he opened his eyes the elevator stopped moving. It only dropped when he closed them. A puddle was growing beneath him. His shirt was sick. He wrapped his arms around his stomach as if to cradle his pain. Bernie's wife moaned for him.

She'd used a birth-control device years earlier, some kind of shield, and it planted something in her that wouldn't let her sleep or eat or work. She fed it painkillers till it became immune to them, like some kind of lifeform bent on survival, and then they'd prescribe new ones. They couldn't pin it down but it had to be in there somewhere. The only way to get it would be to take out everything. She wouldn't let them. Didn't want to be old and hard before her time.

She called her husband at work and moaned at him over the phone. You could hear it rooms away.

A class action was pending.

My fault, Ahmed said. Shouldna hit that pussy so hard. Shit was smokin, still ain't right.

Alright now, Bernie said.

The meat wagon delivered the loser of an argument at the Y. The last word was a screwdriver in the ear, driven to the hilt. The victim had a hard-on.

Musta hit that nerve.

Mighta had a screw loose.

Bet it come out Phillips, L.C. said, and laid odds. Once he came out of the cooler with his arms out in front of him, the palms of his hands turned inward. Healthiest dead bitch I ever saw. He sighed. Sloper found an excuse to stay late, promised to punch their cards when he left.

At least he knew when to laugh. Ahmed couldn't help himself. It got so they wouldn't let him pull back the sheet for the cops anymore. Somebody's loved one, mother or sister, had swung on him. He came back to the locker room giggling, wiped a hand over his face and said, All this was through.

You need to quit, Bernie told him and then

talked about his name. The hell kind of name that was anyway.

L.C. said, It's a Muslim thing.

That ain't me. Moms just put that on me. I deal with Jesus.

Fuck that.

You won't be talkin that shit you get up in fronta that light.

They wore lab coats and called each other Doctor. There was plenty of overtime and Bernie talked about a boat. Or putting down on a house.

Fuck that, Ahmed said. Get the old girl a new box first.

Don't get me started now, Bernie said. L.C. shook his head, afraid to smile. They knew each other's secrets. Sloper wished they'd know his but at least they called him nigger. He was happy there.

Bernie's wife haunted the rooms with her pain. She called Sloper's name. They drowned it out with laughter.

We the horsemens, Ahmed would say.

They stayed after hours, drinking, partying.

Bernie said, It's beer o'clock, but didn't punch his card. Ahmed sat on a slab with a can in one hand, something smoldering in the other. A twelve-pack sitting on a dead man's chest—shotgun wound to the head. Ahmed leaned over and blew smoke into his gaping skull. A gray plume curled up out of the empty, blown-out eye socket.

He hollered into the hole: Wake up motherfucker you don't sleep in my house!

She called his name with an accent. "Slopper!" She was yelling up the shaft. "Slopper! You're stuck? You're okay?" He was wet and shivering.

You made half the bed at a time. You improvised a siderail with two chairs. Rolled the sick person onto her side on the half you weren't making. Rolled half the pullsheet up against her back, then the mattress cover. You straightened the mattress pad. If the bottom bedclothes needed changing, you took a clean mattress cover, half rolled-up, and placed it lengthwise against the roll of dirty bedclothes. You tucked the other half in. You did the same with the pullsheet.

The wheeler at the park was a pimp.

To finish the bed, you moved the pillow and turned the sick person over the rolled bedclothes onto her other side. You pulled through and removed the dirty bedclothes. You pulled through and tucked in the mattress cover, the pullsheet.

When you were transferring her from the bed to the wheelchair you used proper body mechanics. Straight back and knees. Wheels locked and casters turned toward the point of transfer. The caregiver knew her way around wheelchairs, could name makes and models out the corner of her eye. It was funny how many there were in the world once you were involved with one. Like getting a car and noticing how many people drove the same kind.

The pimp in the park rode a Ride-Lite 9000. "More of a woman's chair, I'd say," the caregiver said. A woman pushed it. The pimp would call out to male passersby: "What's going on, bro?" Sometimes they would stop. The three of them would go off somewhere together. Sometimes the customer would even push.

One of the veterans had a power chair. He tooled around the base of the war memorial, a black spire like the steeple of a buried church. Wore dog tags, had a medal pinned to the stump where a knee had been. His chair fluttered with little flags. He wiggled the joystick with the remaining finger and thumb of his remaining arm.

"Action Glide," the caregiver said. "He can go twenty-five, thirty miles before he has to recharge. Five miles an hour. Heavier'n a mother, though."

There was a beep.

He couldn't hear the caregiver. She was over on the esplanade so you couldn't hear her over the half-naked kids screaming in and out of the falling curtain of water. Sloper pushed the woman in the wheelchair around the fountain, the water only misting them. She beeped once, once, once. She must have wanted to get wet and Sloper pushed her inside the curtain and out again. She kept beeping. He dipped in and out of the spray, unpredictably to keep her guessing. One or two now meant the same thing and he pushed her toward the center of the fountain where the water rose. He didn't notice himself pushing harder, they were in the tunnel between where the water went up and where it came down. If you found the right place you didn't get wet. He couldn't hear the caregiver over the water and the children. A small barefoot boy tripped over the footrest and fell sprawling. The cement made a ruthless wet sound. Sloper spun the chair sideways and it tipped. Good thing she was strapped in.

You could hear the caregiver now. You could see her standing blurred just the other side of the curtain of water. In a wheelchair, she was yelling, fifty-four percent of the weight was behind the center of gravity.

If you poked her flesh with your finger, the dimple stayed till you smoothed it out.

He wanted to buy her things—panties, maybe a brassiere—but he couldn't find the nerve to bring them to the counter. Or shove them down his pants. She lay in his mother's bed wearing his underwear, black stockings he'd found in a wastebasket with runs in them. The aunt, if that's what she was, said he should live up there till she rented it out. Or sold the house. She said grown men do not live in basements. She'd already sold the car; Sloper, a grown man, could ride the bus.

He put black tape over her eyes.

He put red lipstick on her mouth so her mouth would put it on him.

He put a chain and padlock on his refrigerator, but he was getting lazy about putting her back on time, what with the stairs. It was getting to be like Cinderella and midnight. Her nose was starting to run, a thin, dirty rivulet. He kissed her, squeezing, and she farted through her mouth. Was it just him, or was there an orange developing in her grayness?

The partner wasn't in his office but you could still hear him. You could smell him. Sloper padded slowly down the narrow hallway. You could hear him better and smell him worse. He was remembering a storm. No, it was something the storm told him. No...

The partner was in the kitchen. "Don't mind me," he said. "Be out of your way in a sec."

He was on his knees, head and shoulders out of sight in the cabinet under the kitchen sink. Sloper heard a click. "I say one thing at a time because I can't say them together. Where was I? Kick me if I'm in your way." Another click.

"Where I was, I was on my way without ever leaving my desk. You could see me coming out over the water, that big dark rolling down from the north, consuming the whole sky. I'm saying like the atmosphere was boiling away into space. Beneath me the lake went pale like blood leaving a face—sort of a milky avocado. Then darker than before, with little white mouths puckering. And all the drivers in their little cars, speeding up, crowding into that shrinking corner of daylight. So I spoke and they hit the shoulder, cleared the way all the way to where she lived. I'd been authorized to institute action and recover the principal. I made a U-turn."

His voice was different, belonged to someone cracked and leathery. String tie. Stetson.

"She lived across town from here but this town isn't big enough. You don't sign a promissory note and then just marry a white man and give yourself to the cause of the less fortunate. Some kind of engineer from what I gather but a judgment had been entered against her. I assumed the debt was valid, I was coming to collect. I raged. Lights winked out down below and I followed that cut black path to her house. Blew in a basement window and crept up the stairs to the kitchen where she'd fed the hungry. She was sitting there with coffee in the only glow left on the block. I'd seen to it. Like she'd set a place for me, giving me everything I needed—candles, the knife block first thing by the kitchen door, her back to me, and the softest music... what treachery it obscures. I won't lie and say I didn't feel the loss of her when she ground herself against me, coming out of herself all over me, out of her throat, heart and belly. It was only by chance her breast came to be in my hand, but a storm can't help what it does, being a storm, even if there was a man and a child left in that house, and real love you could almost smell. Taste.

"Saw the little one first, come down scared by the thunder or some of what I hadn't been able to stop all of, or to say goodnight to her mother—scream goodbye to her mother. Even in the dark and especially in the last moments of her eight or nine years she was beautiful with the same color of honey in her hair and skin, flecks of it in her eyes, and it was them I made my way to to stop her screaming. I never hurt her, just kept her cries in a corner while he came down the stairs like it was the fresh silence that brought him, bringing a rumble of his own. Passed us right by. Then I heard him there in the kitchen, confronted with the consequences of default, and I headed for the nearest way out, but he saw me before a decent interval had passed. He said something. I don't think he saw who I had in my hands, too much grief or too much dark in his eye. I turned and lifted her to show him, and his hand blazed with what I didn't know he had, made a sharp report that is nothing next to a storm but enough to splash her brains onto my face—I'm saying the taste of them—so that she wasn't a kid anymore but something I'd been given to use, truthfully the best weapon I could have hoped for. He was close enough to catch it and go down in a heap when he did.

"He was over. What he'd seen and done was the dark at the end of the tunnel, but don't think I could have walked away then, that it wouldn't have mattered if I'd just left him there. He only wanted the one piece of mercy left in that house that night and I obliged with the gun he'd dropped, one last sound I hid inside my voice like everything else, the sound of the death trapped inside him breaking loose...bang! It was an effort to collect a debt." Sloper heard a thump. "Holy shit."

Had he bumped his head on the trap, too? "Don't even get me started on those mountains." His voice sounded familiar again. "You wouldn't believe how they creep up on you. Just look out the window tomorrow and see how much bigger they are. Next thing you know: boom! Right on top of you. They're slick that way."

Sloper hadn't seen any mountains. Maybe you only could from the partner's office.

"Black," the Client Manager said.

"Too much iron," Sloper said.

"Pale, greasy."

"Liver problem. Or gall bladder."

"Hard," the Client Manager said. She had concerns. Whenever there were problems, Services just got slammed. Even when it wasn't really their domain. They'd get raked.

"Hard and dry."

"Constipation," Sloper said.

The Client Manager looked at the woman in the wheelchair. "This just isn't like you."

In a way it didn't matter, the caregiver had said. In the long run they could do what they wanted without her approval, but it would be better to stay on good terms. The Client Manager knew her way around Medicare and could help them get things,

patient-handling devices, like the stairlift the woman
in the wheelchair rode belted into a gray upholstered
seat, rising at twenty-two feet per minute on an ex-
truded aluminum track.

"Third of a horsepower," the caregiver said.
"Rack-and-pinion suspension." She called the obstruction sensor the cowcatcher. Next would be the
machine that stimulated the muscles with electrodes
to prevent atrophy, because you never knew. Or the
mattress that circulated air through a series of pockets
with a small motor. You wouldn't have to rotate her
every four hours then, wash and lubricate the shiny
red spots, pad them with flannel or cotton. Or make
a sheepskin. Sloper could make a sheepskin if he had
to. He could make a backrest from a cardboard box,
silence a door with a sponge and duct tape. He could
make a bed with mitered corners.

"Urine?"

"Boiling water and Lysol," Sloper said carefully.
"Rinse with warm water."

The caregiver had had a talk with Sloper about
personal hygiene. She brought up the matter of the

van. She did not feel they should have to pay for a new radiator. The Client Manager would make an inquiry.

"It just isn't like you to rush into things," she told the woman in the wheelchair. She was concerned.

She asked Sloper the Ten Questions.

She asked him other things—about his mother's social security, about his current employment. Did he know he would have to give up his job? she concerned. That what he was getting into, he was getting into twenty-four/seven, three hundred and sixty-five?

"Yeah," Sloper said. "Yes ma'am."

"But marriage?" She kept looking at the woman in the wheelchair.

For a while you couldn't go into the cubicle on 24. Two yellow plastic strips formed an X across the entrance. Warnings were printed on them. Sloper pushed his cart past.

Even after the X came down, people came and went. They would hear about the girl who had the cubicle before them and they would not come back. Finally a nameplate appeared on the cubicle. Some guy. He tacked his own pictures up, left his own reading material lying around, generated his own brand of waste. Sloper never saw him—he must have gotten his work done on time. He never left anything to eat.

Upstairs they were dancing on his head. He'd promised to look into it.

First he got her out of the Maytag, carried her upstairs and set her in the wing chair in the living room, moisture beading up on her like a can in a soft drink commercial.

He liked licking the dew off her.

He crossed her legs. His tongue came across something on her thigh, a rough raised patch like a rash, maybe a fungus from the refrigerator. It wasn't the first. He would go at them with a toothbrush.

The ceiling thudded and crashed like the party or whatever it was was going to come down on his head. The bass thumped in his chest. It didn't really bother him all that much but he'd promised them next door.

He poured Listerine down her throat.

Her breath was getting to him but at least there was no bloat to her that he could see, no intestines pushing out of her mouth, anus, her openings. The steps were getting to him but he couldn't move her to his mother's refrigerator.

He put her in bed and climbed the front stairs. It had been years. They'd grown steep and narrow, the passage high and musty with secondhand air, the stillborn warmth of a breath held too long.

The party sounded different on its side than it did from beneath it. Nobody answered his knock. He went back down and rang the outside doorbell. At least he could say he'd tried.

When he got back up the door was open the width of a bleary-eyed girl's face. "Hi," Sloper said.

She looked him up and down, swaying. "Wanna watch sockey?"

He didn't understand. "You don't live here, do you?"

She mouthed something he couldn't hear over the music and went away, leaving the door open. Sloper waited. He heard shouting, smelled beer, incense or perfumed sweat, a burnt smell that took him back to the morgue. They turned the music down but nobody came. He went in.

He was in a narrow hall. The light was out except for what was coming from under the bathroom door. He knew the layout. He passed the bedroom. The door was open and the darkness inside groaned, smelled rank and intimate. He knew the layout but not his way around up here.

Somebody came down the hall. They tried to get out of each other's way and only made it worse. "Okay, let's dance," a young man's voice said.

"I live downstairs," Sloper said. "Is the guy who lives here up here?"

"He's sort of out of it," the young man said. "Watch some sockey? Have a coldie."

He went back down the hall. Sloper followed, passing through what was meant to be the dining room. A lamp sat on the floor in a corner, the shade glowing a dim orange. A boy lay on the floor nearby. Next to his head was a bowl filled with something thick and chunky. He rolled his eyes to Sloper. His mouth was open, moving, making a choking sound. A pair of legs stood by. Sloper did not look to see who they belonged to.

"Too much is never enough," the legs said.

The living room was bright and noisy and everyone was crowded at the entranceway. Sloper stepped up and looked over all the shoulders.

He hadn't realized how big the living room was without furniture. The hardwood floor was bare, stripped and scarred, gouged. Smoke hung like gauze. Four young men stood there with sawed-off hockey sticks.

Two of them were shirtless. One of them had on what looked like war paint, and fresh scratches on his back and chest, except that they were deeper and darker than scratches. Furrows. The other skin had a gut, a kerchief tied over his mouth.

"Does he really pee on it first?" someone wondered to someone. As if for Sloper's benefit.

One of the shirts had a brown cloth patch covering an eye. Sloper realized the color was dried blood. He saw the same color on the blade of one of the sticks, which was curved and pointed like that of a scythe. Some kid keeping score on the wall with a piece of chalk. The wall was covered with old scores, crossed out, and other writings. Someone else was balling up a pair of sweatsocks and wrapping them in duct tape. Its predecessor lay at his feet, battered and ruptured beyond use.

There weren't many girls. One of them looked at Sloper. "Who do you say? Cannibals or Gladiators?"

"I don't know. Is one of them the tenant?"

A cold can was pressed into his hand. "Enjoy," the young man said. "What do you think?"

"I don't know," Sloper said. He didn't like to raise his voice. "It's getting a little loud up here for me. Down there. Your party."

The guy looked disappointed. He looked like maybe he wasn't so young. "It's outta my hands."

"I need to talk to the tenant."

"New sock!"

The guy turned away. "Down the hall."

The bedroom door was closed now. Sloper knocked and nobody answered. "I just came up to ask you to turn down the noise." A silence he put his ear to. Whoever was inside was trying to whisper but their voices were too deep not to carry. One was young and one was older. Sloper listened for a girl. "It's not for me," he said. "It's for the neighbors."

There was a commotion down the hall, a big crash and then a cry as of great pain. The crowd uproared, repulsed to satisfaction.

"Thank you."

You couldn't expect immediate results.

He lay on his back, got an arm under her shoulders, and rolled her onto him. Rubbed her hand warm, then pushed and pulled on himself with it. Squeezed her behind. Her flesh gave but it no longer gave back. Like soft putty, but you couldn't call it soggy. The lights were off.

A couple of people left but they came right back. Sloper heard them on the back stairs, the rattle of paper bags. The thumping had stopped for the time being.

He'd cross-tied her wrists with one of her stockings and slipped them behind his neck like a yoke. He hooked her legs over his shoulders, thick calves flattening against his shoulder blades. Still had trouble finding it in the dark, but he no longer needed spit or grease.

The voices multiplied, the music rose to the occasion. His hips banged against her thighs. He got his hands under the small of her back and lifted her towards him, lifted her breasts toward his mouth, a taste like pennies. Her back arched and her head hung back, the back of her head almost touching her spine. He lay down on top of her, his heart beating enough for them both. She farted.

The ceiling shook.

It was no use.

He just couldn't get gripped there anymore. He swung her arms up, slid back and out, turned her over. Light entered the room, distorted rectangular patches stretching over the walls, bending at corners.

Headlights in the driveway. No one was supposed to block the driveway.

Sloper peeked from the edge of the bedroom window shade. A police car. Two uniformed shapes emerged and headed for the back of the house. The stairs, the weary climb. He got back into bed.

You could hear them at the back door upstairs. Must have been using the butt of a flashlight, or a night stick. Then you could hear all the noise that much more, invading the air over the back porch. Somebody yelled and the music faded.

If they wanted to talk to him, wouldn't they have knocked on his door first?

The darkness overhead was quiet and reasonable, the footsteps calm, considerate. He'd gotten started again without realizing it. He licked an ear, sniffed her lank hair. The tip of his cock kept bumping something spongy that hadn't been there before. He was running out of holes—wasn't he only kidding when he'd thought about making a new one?

Somebody got loud. A scuffle. Footsteps pounded across the ceiling from the front of the apartment to the back. A loud crash from the kitchen. Shouting, more scuffling. The scuffling ended but the shouting didn't. Sloper interrupted himself, caught his breath. Things were happening too fast and then too slow. He heard them coming down the back steps now, several pairs of feet, nice and easy. A girl shouted above them: "Where's your probable cause?" Sloper couldn't make out the answer. It went back and forth.

"Don't worry," she shouted then. "We'll meet you at the station."

He didn't want to have to wait. The music stayed off, there were only voices and footsteps. Someone stomped, sounded like they were cursing. People went down the back steps and came back up. A neighbor's door opened and closed. There were exchanges. A car started on the street but you could still hear the police radio in the driveway—why did it have to take so long? He couldn't wait. Just like at the morgue, he couldn't help himself. Didn't want to. He shook himself all out and then fell asleep with his mouth on hers, tasting himself, breathing in and out of her. He dreamed she was kissing him back, her tongue tickling his. He woke up and she still was, but their mouths were apart.

Something was crawling on his tongue.

He tried to spit it out and it got stuck on his lip. He plucked it off and crushed it between his fingers. He flicked the bed lamp on just long enough to see another one squirming on her pillow. The police were gone.

Someone was knocking at the back door.

Must have left her out of the cold once too long. Or they might have been there from the start, just crawling up all that time from her belly.

The knocking stopped, gathered itself, came back harder. Sloper crept to the kitchen doorway but didn't go in. The light on the landing was burned out, you couldn't see who was at the door but they were a group. One of them spoke.

"Bullshit," another said. "He never goes anywhere." More pounding. Sloper scratched his tongue. They couldn't see him but he wouldn't go in the kitchen.

There was some sort of discussion: "Can they charge him?"

Something you couldn't hear.

Something in the first degree.

"Leave him alone," a young man said. "They said it was someone else."

"Hell yeah, they say that." Trying not to shout. "He's been like a father to us."

Sloper wondered if the tenant was out there. He should put her back. He backed away from the kitchen.

"I'll huff and I'll puff, motherfucker." There seemed to be sobbing.

"You're drunk."

"Lucky I'm not sober." The door rattled. "Don't be a scaredy, open up. You know who that was you narked on?"

Sloper went back to his mother's bed. The voice seemed to follow him. It was loud but suddenly quite reasonable. "Come on, open up. I just want to talk. Man to man. You can't hide in there forever."

Forget Listerine. He needed something stronger.

Sloper was named Janitor of the Month.

The whole shift gathered in the cafeteria.

Lunchtime was extended by half an hour. There were three kinds of pizza and a slide show of the new sprinkler system. When the lights came back on the Regional Manager rose, a dapper, distinguished-looking man, but mushmouthed. He always sounded slightly drunk.

"Lays and gelman," he said. He had a surprise: the award had been increased from a twenty-five-dollar gift certificate to a fifty-dollar check. And contrary to rumor, he said, the increase had been in the works long before Silicon Valley.

The top dogs took turns making speeches. The Building Manager stood and struggled not to repeat what his predecessor had said. Then he found a riff and emphasized that the award was the building's way of demonstrating appreciation and support, that its faith in the service was undiminished despite a recent incident, the details of which he felt it unnecessary to go into because everybody made mistakes. Sloper recalled an architect's red face, a set of blueprints mistaken for recycling—unless he was talking about something else—but anyway, pineapple had no business on pizza and the second time he went up he got two slices each of the other two kinds.

The District Manager had another surprise: the service had contracted with the building going up across the street—nearing completion, as a matter of fact. The new building was asking the service for its best, most experienced employees, some of whom might be sitting in that very room. Pay would be commensurate.

The worst part was having to stand up, tell everyone your name, how long you'd been with the service, and how long you'd been in the building. Everybody got their turn. Some people had names like Fabio or Dung and thick, incomprehensible accents, and a couple of times you really had to hold it in.

The decision was based on attitude, attendance, appearance, and quality of service as evaluated by inspection.

Sloper was recognized.

The supervisor pronounced his name correctly but he still had to be nudged into realizing he'd been chosen. A Polaroid was taken, Sloper flanked by his supervisor and the District Manager on one side, the Regional Manager and the Building Manager on the other. While the picture developed things loosened up. People spoke in their own tongues. One of the Africans shared a long-awaited photograph of her homeland—a family standing in front of a bungalow with part of a station wagon.

"What a byooaful country," the Regional Manager elided, but it could have been Indiana for all anybody knew.

Sloper's unaccustomed smile faded in through a field of whiteness, the check held up at his chest, the gross amount compensated for payroll deduction.

He hadn't told anyone he was leaving.

There was time for a brief Q&A. People raised their hands and the Regional Manager pointed at them. Bell lifted his arm. He tried to use some big words but what he wanted to know was why the day porter made more than anyone on the evening shift.

All the food was soft all the days of the regimen. You had to make it softer in the blender. Half-cups and third-cups. Powdered milk, strained bananas, scrambled eggs, hot cream.

Someone wanted to talk to him.

"Mom's heart broke when I left for school. And worse. Drove her to become some kind of groupie. She'd call and name the stars she was spreading for backstage, she missed me so bad. Motivational speakers, eulogists. She lost it and said, The gods are frowning upon us. Next thing you know I set myself on fire lighting a cigarette. She sent out familiars, little dark animals to spy on me. Her love was always with me—I've got the scratches to prove it. But I had promises to myself to keep. Summers I worked my way through doing inventory in fabric stores. City to city, she'd track me down. Tell them shut up with the numbers! she'd yell over the phone. Even after law school, after I'd arrived and unlisted myself, she called. I'd hear street noise, hospital PA, billiards, echo of unfurnished rooms. It might have been a client, I had to pick up. Phones just make me a nervous wreck anymore, like maybe I fought in some dirty old war with the ultimate booby trap, the one that took you out from the waist down, triggered by lifting a receiver. Let me tell you: it would have been an honor."

The door was open. You could hear a whir like spinning metal.

"I hated it when she cried but she was just so tired of being alone. She just wanted me to sing 'Honey' one more time, but something took my voice whenever it was her. The calls dwindled in number, spread themselves apart in time. After a while she wouldn't say anything, just made a mewing sound into the receiver."

A big hollow click that was not the Dictaphone.

"But the last time we talked, how cheerful she sounded, how well-adjusted. She heard my excuses with this accommodating chuckle. It was terrifying. I'd known her all my life.

"Even now I can sense her voice, inching toward me through the wires. Goddamn mountains right behind her."

You could hear the whir and then the click. Sloper was almost off the floor.

"Enclosed you will find a rough copy of the

proposed will. There are more affidavits to be attached but I prefer to hear your reply first. Until
then, I remain

They asked him about the carpet roll.

He said anyone could take it. It was allowed.

But, they asked, why had he bothered to carry
it at all? They showed him himself on tape.

He thought he could carry it down to the car,
but it turned out to be heavier than he thought.
So...

They asked him nothing else. They sighed.

Sloper's replacement went through the pockets
of the yellow plastic apron. He found a bulky foil-
wrapped package. "What's this?"

Sloper started to reach for it, then shrugged and
said, "Garbage."

"You mean trash." The replacement dropped it
in the barrel. He was also a security guard, graveyard
at some bank. "Chapter 7," he explained, "11, 13, and
some more they wrote just for me." Not to mention a

tricky divorce, but sometimes you just had to bite the bullet. He was a survivor. "Hell, I lived under a truck camper in someone's back forty for a year without them knowing it. Ate nothing but rolled oats."

You could tell it was getting to him. He would be talking to you, then would stop in mid-sentence and stare at you until you felt like a blank spot. When he came back he was on a destroyer in the South China Sea.

"Must've been rough," Sloper said.

"Loved every minute of it. Wartime Navy was a blast, it was peacetime that made you crazy. They were in your shit every minute, gave you a rash, nothing to do but drink and fuck with jarheads." He shook his head. "Wasn't much doing after Saigon though, unless you count Pakistan."

Sloper showed him where everything was. They trashed floors together. The replacement disappeared for a while, came back with a pack of cigarettes and a dirty magazine. Said he was on break. He had a habit of flinging the barrel down the aisles instead of pushing it. Sloper made him stop.

"Just trying to save us some steps," he said.

"Jesus Chrysler, this is boring. How do you occupy your mind?"

Sloper showed him the plastic cube. "No batteries, huh? I'll think about it. You say everything's paid for?"

"What do you mean?"

"What about, you know——?"

"What about what?"

"Anytime you want it, huh?"

Sloper thought. "Anytime."

"And you don't have to work. So how's this van running?"

"Hot."

"Not good. Suppose you're driving around and you want to stop somewhere for a taste. Just a lousy boilermaker, we're talking fifteen minutes. You might as well leave her in the van—what's she gonna say?—but if it's running hot, no AC. See what I'm getting at? You know what happens to dogs. Better—" The replacement broke off and stared.

"You take the bitch to the park," he said when he came back.

"Huh."

"You take her to the park. The bitch is in heat but you're a kid, you want to play, explore. You leave her tied to a tree. She'll be okay, she's a Husky-Lab mix—they don't get much bigger than that. But when you come back her you-know-what's all pulled inside out, dragging on the ground. The question is, if she's a Husky-Lab mix, how big did he have to be that did that to her?"

He broke off again down in the trash room. Sloper waited but he kept staring and not saying anything.

Sloper went and got a drink of water and came back.

The replacement gave him a lift. There was a hole in the floor of his car and you could see the road streaming below. It didn't occur to Sloper until they were halfway there that it could happen while they were driving. At an intersection reasonably close to home, he blurted, "This is fine" and jumped out, barely shutting the door.

His replacement yelled, "Remember what happens to dogs!"

All the lights were out. They were out next door because the caregiver and the woman in the wheelchair turned in at nine. At his house because the people upstairs had moved out. The new owners gave Sloper till the end of the month but he'd be gone before then.

He looked at the window above the side porch, looked forward to riding the little chair up past it—his weight fell within its rated load. He looked forward to looking through the window and watching his old life drift down from left to right into the past, from where he now imagined rising up to her sickroom with a beer in his hand or the plastic cube, on his way to whatever it was he had to do.

A washcloth for soap and another to rinse.

You called it a wellroom, not a sickroom.

When he switched on the light in the foyer, he noticed the basement door was ajar. He pushed it shut and then remembered pushing it shut before he'd gone to work. And locking it. At least he thought so. Could have been the new owners. They hadn't taken actual possession but she let them come and go as they pleased.

Sloper switched on the basement light and went downstairs, not quite sure what it was he was making sure of. He moved slowly, and slowly saw that the window was still intact. The washer and dryer. Around the furnace. Musty brick, the shower curtain drawn. The refrigerator still there, but not the chain and padlock. Their absence kept jumping out at him. The blank white door would recede and then jump back out. It made the handle hard to reach for.

She was still inside. Duct tape still covered her mouth.


There was a message on her chest and belly. Hard to make out, maybe lipstick. Mrs. something. It was hard to make out because the appliance bulb had been removed, but Sloper didn't realize that till the basement light went out.

The chain rattled.

Stifled laughter or maybe a sneeze.

He didn't see any point in asking who was there. A flickering. He turned his head and a round patch of light appeared and disappeared on the wall behind him.

A voice said, "How about a coldie?" Sloper turned in the direction of the voice and got a light in his face, as blinding as the dark. The bulb shattered against his head with a pop. Didn't even hurt.

If the nails were thick and tough you soaked them first. You washed the hair with a waterless shampoo. If a sick person had her own teeth, you held her mouth open with a spoon when you brushed and flossed them. If she used a catheter the opening to the bladder had to be kept clean. You kept half of her covered while you did the other half—a sick person had shame even if you were married to her.

His arms were no help. He tried to crawl over the bulging cement, look for the wind he'd lost, but they'd gone to sleep. Something to do with the knot of nerves in the center of his chest. Solar something. Learned it at the morgue. He heard the click of the cups and balls.

They were standing on his hand. Someone lifted him out of the blackness by his hair. A dim patch of face. "Ready for that cold one?" Something warm backing up in his throat. Sloper coughed, he didn't mean to spit. A sound of disgust and he was dropped. Another foot in his ribs.

"Oogh," he said.

"Goddamn right," they said, out of breath. "Someone's going through the trouble of beating your ass... You could at least cooperate."

"Payback's a bitch."

"I bet it's tight."

"What do you douche with, formaldehyde?"

Someone sighed. "Let's not take all night."

Dinner of the last day of the regimen was strained chicken blenderized with pureed carrots. For feces you soaked in cold water. A quarter-cup and a quarter-cup.

"Oogh," they said. "Uhn."

Bernie bought a boat to sail away from his wife. He said he'd take Sloper fishing but he never called.

Cans opening, beers maybe. "Are we having fun yet?"

"Think of it as a learning experience."

"He should be a genius by now. What'd you get?"

"Three for three."

"Bullshit, lemme see."

"Whups." Shattering of plastic. The bearings bouncing and rolling on the cement.

"What about those mixers on the east side? Think that's him?"

"Fucking mutts. We should shake his hand."

"Maybe there's a reward."

"Fuck that, let's get going."

"We should shake *our* hand."

"What if there's a reward?"

He tasted something awful. Warm and bitter, not beer at all.

"Happy honeymoon!"

His back was against solid cold. He didn't know if his eyes were swollen shut but he couldn't make the dark go away. It wouldn't let him move. She had an arm over his shoulder, her face pressed against his. His knees were drawn up and she straddled him, her weight making it hard to breathe. His ribs killed him like crazy when he did. Overhead and to his left he felt metal, slick with frost. The same to his right, but there was more to it. His hand recognized the shelving.

He heard a voice, a muffled falsetto. It sounded almost like his own but spoke in a dead language that was familiar only in part.


You massaged thin cords of muscle to prevent atrophy. Just in case. Never took an escalator. Dusted the bedpan with talcum powder.

You presented food to the strong side of the mouth, and you never forced.

CPSIA information can be obtained
at www.ICGtesting.com
Printed in the USA
FSOW02n0916200415
6502FS

9 780963 753618